I Love Planes!

BY **Philemon Sturges**

ILLUSTRATED BY **Shari Halpern**

HarperCollinsPublishers

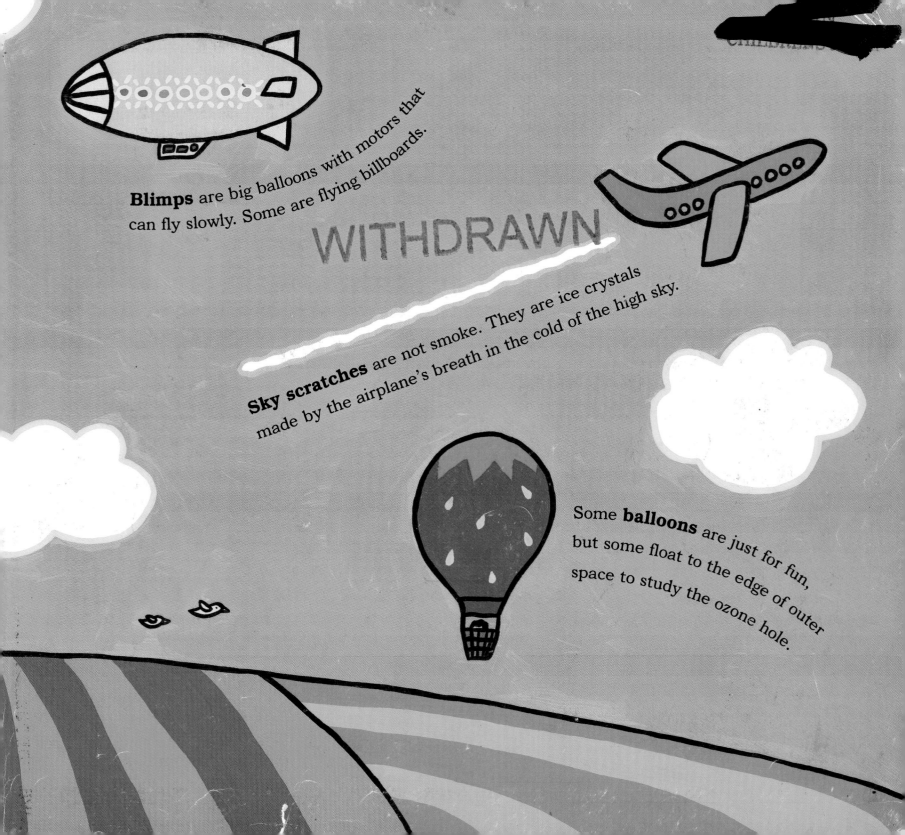

Blimps are big balloons with motors that can fly slowly. Some are flying billboards.

Sky scratches are not smoke. They are ice crystals made by the airplane's breath in the cold of the high sky.

Some **balloons** are just for fun, but some float to the edge of outer space to study the ozone hole.

To Phoebe, who sings as I
search for a simpler word
—P.S.

For Owen Samuel
—S.H.

I Love Planes!
Text copyright © 2003 by Philemon Sturges
Illustrations copyright © 2003 by Shari Halpern
Printed in the U.S.A. All rights reserved. www.harperchildrens.com
Library of Congress Cataloging-in-Publication Data Sturges, Philemon.
I love planes! / by Philemon Sturges ; illustrated by Shari Halpern. p.   cm.
Summary: A child celebrates his love of planes by naming his favorite kinds and their
notable characteristics.   ISBN 0-06-028898-1 — ISBN 0-06-028899-X (lib. bdg.)
[1. Airplanes—Fiction.] I. Halpern, Shari, ill. II. Title.   PZ7.S94124 Iae 2003
[E]—dc21   2001026483   CIP   AC
1 2 3 4 5 6 7 8 9 10
❖
First Edition

Planes, planes, planes! I like planes.

I want to fly up high and scratch the sky.

Or float to the moon

in a big balloon.

Or blink like a blimp at the ball game.

I like to loop the loop

and power dive,

And hover,

and soar,

Or shoot from a boat with an ear-blasting roar.

I want to land on the sea and not get wet,

Then zoom to Grandpa's

in my jumbo jet!

But most of all, I want to fly

to where stars twinkle in the sky . . .

And visit Mom.

Planes, planes, planes!

I
LOVE
planes!

The **space shuttles** are rocketed into space, where they float like the moon. Then they glide home.

A **passenger jet** can carry several hundred people halfway around the world in less than a day.

A catapult launches **jet fighters** from the deck of an aircraft carrier.